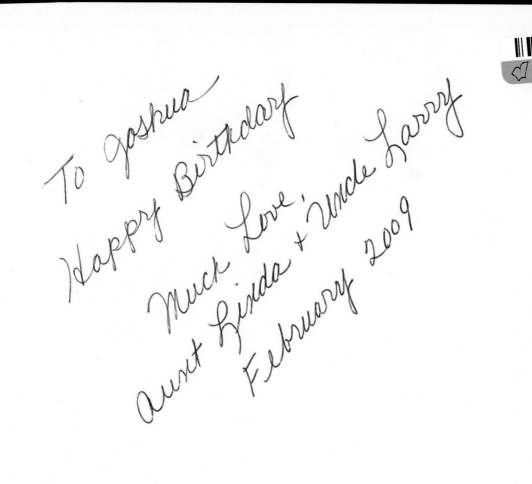

To Joshua

Happy Birthday

Much Love,

Aunt Linda + Uncle Larry

February 2009

Disney's Storybook Collection

VOLUME 2

Disney
PRESS

New York

TABLE OF CONTENTS

TABLE OF CONTENTS

DISNEY ✦ PIXAR

a bug's life

THE QUEST FOR THE ONE BIG THING

Princess Dot was eagerly waiting for the circus bugs to return to the ant colony for the harvest. Finally, Dot checked the calendar and realized that the twelve days of the harvest would begin the next day!

On the first day of the harvest, Dot set out alone, not sure what 1 ant could do. While Dot was sitting on a blade of grass, a dewdrop knocked her onto a big sticky thing. Sweet goo covered her legs. This One Big Thing would feed the colony for the winter! But Dot could not lift it, so she hurried home.

The next day, Dot told her sister, Queen Atta, about the One Big Sticky Thing. The **2** ants set off to see what they could do.

The One Big Thing looked even bigger and stickier. They tried to lift it, then push it, but it would not budge. Disappointed, they returned to the colony.

On the third day of the harvest, Heimlich arrived. He ADORED food. When Dot described the One Big Gooey Thing, he insisted that the **3** of them depart at once.

They tried to pull it, but it would not move. They gave up and went home.

On the fourth day, all the circus bugs arrived. Dot was sure that **4** of them could carry the One Big Thing. She secretly asked Gypsy to join them.

They pushed and pulled with no luck. Gypsy even tried a magic trick, but the One Big Thing just sat there.

Discouraged, they headed home.

On the morning of the fifth day, Slim overheard Heimlich talking in his sleep about a tasty, gooey secret. Dot filled him in, and the **5** of them went off.

This time, they tried rolling the One Big Thing, but with no luck. Once again they returned to the colony.

On the sixth day, Dot decided they needed Manny the magician's help. The **6** harvesters departed.

Shouts of "hocus-pocus" and "abracadabra" did not move it. Miracle dust and powerful powders floating in the air could not even budge it. They leaned against the One Big Thing, then shuffled home.

The next day, Queen Atta told everyone about the One Big Thing. All the bugs began talking at once. Flik appeared and quieted everyone. He suggested that **7** harvesters try again.

They spent the whole time shooing flies away from the One Big Thing. Then, the weary bugs returned home.

On the eighth day, Dot *almost* gave up. But Dim flexed his wings and said the One Big Tasty Thing wasn't too big for him! So the **8** harvesters set out.

Dim pushed while the others pulled. The One Big Thing did not budge. With no energy left, they headed home.

On the ninth day, Rosie cracked her silk whip and marched **9** of them to the One Big Thing.

This time, they lifted it off the ground and began to inch forward. Blades of grass twisted around their ankles until they collapsed. No one was hurt, but they returned to the colony, defeated again.

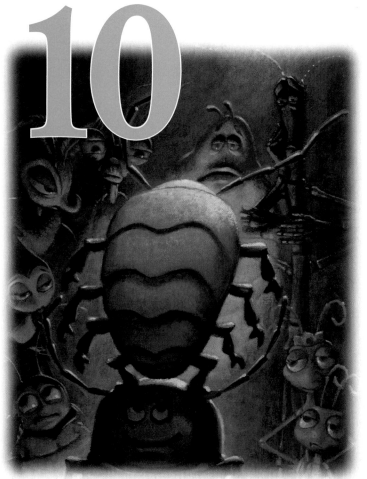

The next morning, when Dot suggested that **10** harvesters might be the right number, Atta just rolled her eyes. Even Tuck and Roll's comic imitation of Hopper could not cheer them up.

With only two days left for harvesting, Dot wondered if they would ever get the One Big Thing. She tried to think of a plan.

On the eleventh day, Dot was going to make a final attempt to get the One Big Thing. Anyone who wanted to be *truly helpful* could come, too, so **11** harvesters

marched off.

They managed to prop the One Big Thing on its end. But no one knew what to do next, so they curled up under some leaves and fell asleep.

Meanwhile, back at the colony, Flik rushed out of
the lab, shouting for everyone to come see his new
invention. The colony was empty. He noticed a well-worn

path leading away
from the anthill and
set out. Flik found
his friends sleeping
near the One Big
Thing. He woke
them up to describe
his new invention.

Flik wiggled his legs like mechanical arms and accidentally backed up right into the One Big Thing! He bumped it hard enough to send it careening, end over sticky end, down the hill. It catapulted off a rock, flew high in the air, and disappeared from sight.

All **12** of them chased after it.

The One Big Thing made a sticky, gooey, honey-glazed landing right outside the colony entrance. There was more than enough food for the winter. And there was even dessert!

All because everyone had worked together to get the **One Big Thing**.

THE FINAL STAND

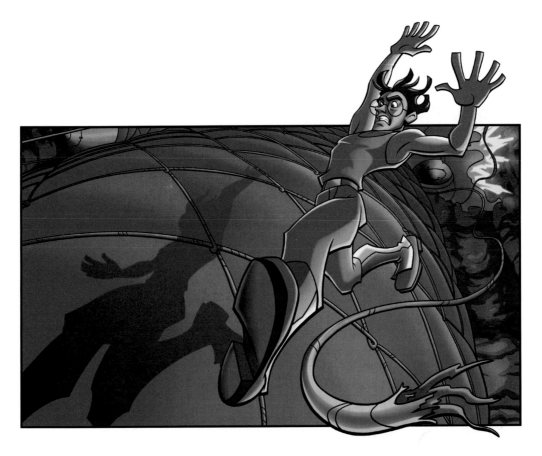

Milo Thatch had unknowingly led the villainous Commander Rourke to the lost city of Atlantis. Now Rourke had stolen the Crystal, the Atlanteans' life force, with Princess Kida crystallized inside it.

"In times of danger," said the king of Atlantis, "the

Crystal will choose a host, one of royal blood, to protect itself and its people."

But who would protect Atlantis now that the Crystal had been taken away? Milo had come along on this expedition as a linguist and a cartographer, not as a soldier. He looked down at the small crystal in his hand—the king's own crystal. Then Milo rose to his feet and strode out of the room.

Outside the palace, the expedition crew and the Atlanteans watched as Milo climbed onto an Atlantean stone-fish vehicle. "I'm going after Rourke," said Milo. He inserted the king's crystal into the vehicle's keyhole, and in a flash it rose off the ground. Milo had to get the Crystal back to save Atlantis!

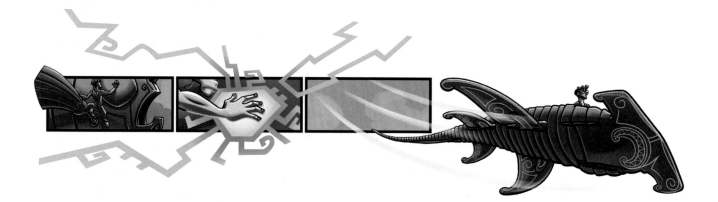

Everyone rushed to other stone-fish vehicles—Aktiraks, Ketaks, and Martags—and started them up. Even Milo's fellow crew members Audrey, Dr. Sweet, Mole, and Vinny joined in. The new Atlantean armada was on the move!

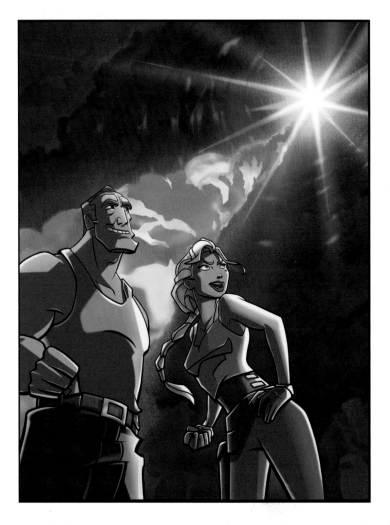

Ka-boom!

Inside a nearby volcano shaft, a cannon blew a hole in the top of the volcano. This was Rourke's escape route to the surface world. He smiled evilly at his lieutenant, Helga.

"I love it when I win," he snarled.

Behind Rourke, a trooper removed the top of a water tanker. Inside was a hot-air balloon called the gyro-evac, which automatically began to inflate. The trooper attached chains to secure the transport pod containing Kida, the crystallized princess, to the gyro-evac. Then Rourke and Helga climbed aboard, and the gyro-evac began to rise.

Milo and the armada

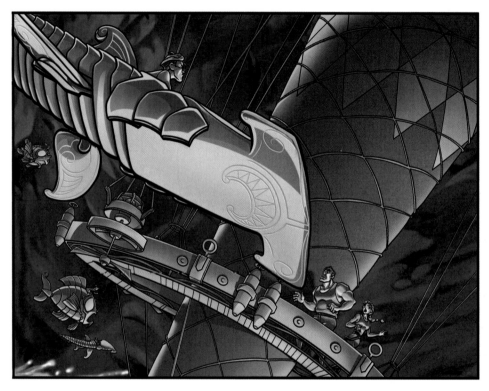

emerged from an underground cave and spotted Helga

and Rourke making their getaway.

"There they are!" Milo shouted.

Rourke's troopers opened fire. The Atlanteans

shot back with spears and bows and arrows. The
battle raged.

Then Vinny accidentally leaned on a button
on his Martag. Out shot a laser beam,
taking out one of the troopers'
trucks!

"Okay, now things are getting
good!" Vinny shouted.

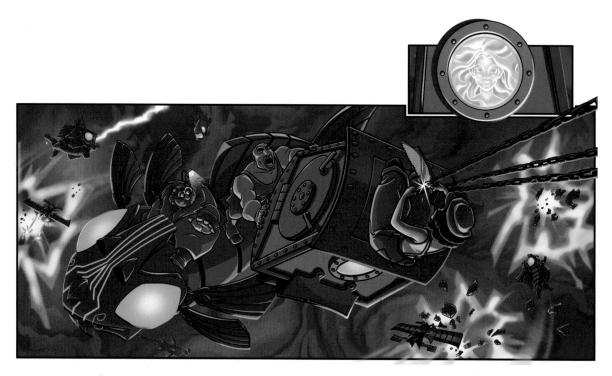

Audrey, Dr. Sweet, and Mole veered away from the battle. They couldn't let Rourke escape with Kida! They guided their Martag until it hovered under the princess pod. Then Audrey scrambled up and tried to saw through the chains. But they were too thick!

Meanwhile, Milo steered his Aktirak straight at the gyro-evac. When he was a few feet from the balloon, he leaped through the air, barely catching hold of the netting that covered the gyro-evac. At the very same moment, his Aktirak— now without a driver—ripped a large hole in the balloon.

"We're losing altitude!" Rourke cried. He had to lighten the load. When Helga's back was turned, he pushed her over the side. Helga grabbed the railing and swung herself back up, but Rourke managed to toss her out of the gyro-evac again—this time for good.

"Nothing personal," Rourke called out to her.

Seconds later, Milo swung down from above, knocking Rourke off his feet.

But Rourke recovered quickly. "You're a bigger pain in the neck than I would have ever thought possible," he said. He

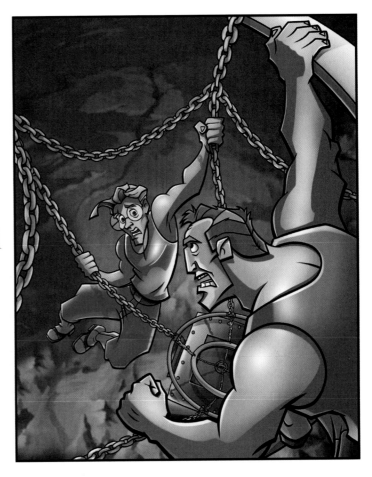

kicked Milo through the side railing. Luckily, Milo caught hold of the chains that held the princess pod.

Suddenly, a flare tore into the balloon, setting it on fire. On the ground, Helga lowered her flare gun. "Nothing personal," she echoed.

Rourke grabbed an ax from the emergency casing in the gyro-evac and climbed down after Milo.

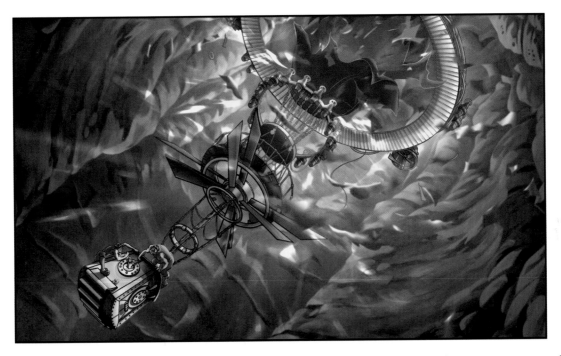

Rourke swung the ax. Milo ducked. The ax struck the pod, shattering the window. Desperately, Milo plucked out a shard of glass that glowed with the Crystal's energy. Then, as Rourke grabbed Milo by the throat, Milo slashed Rourke's arm with the shard.

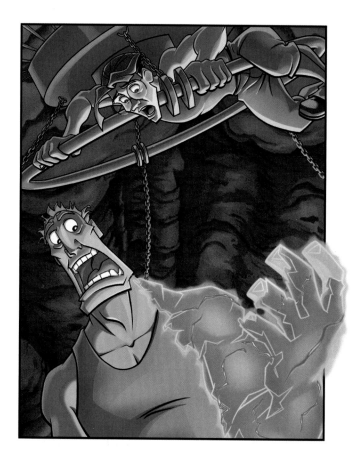

Rourke's grip loosened. A blue light shot up his arm, changing his flesh to crystal. The Crystal recognized Rourke's evil, turning him an angry red, then black. Then Rourke hardened into a crystallized statue.

When he got in the way of the gyro-evac's massive spinning blades, his crystalline body shattered.

Then Milo heard a snap. The chains had broken, and the princess pod plunged to the ground. Milo jumped down after it! He pushed the pod out of harm's way, only seconds before the gyro-evac crashed to the ground and exploded.

The force of the explosion reached underground.

The volcano was going to erupt!

They had to get out of there! Quickly, Milo wrapped one end of a chain around the pod while Audrey and Vinny attached the other end to the back of their Martag. They outran the fiery lava and raced back to Atlantis.

In the center plaza of Atlantis, Audrey gently
lowered the princess pod to the ground. Milo began to
pry it open with a spear. Suddenly, the walls of the pod
flew off. Kida hovered in the air, glowing with the life
energy of the city.

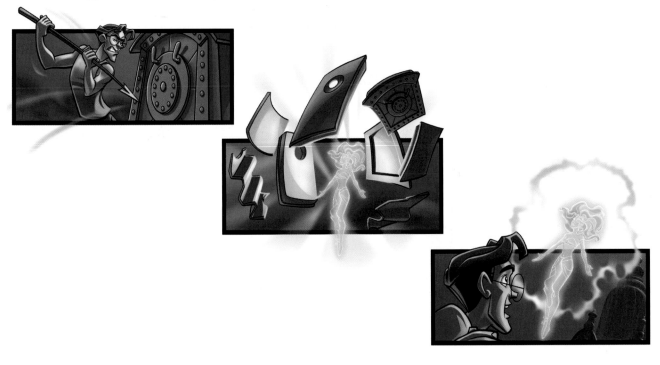

Beneath the plaza, the King Stones—statues of past Atlantean kings—also began to glow, brought to life by Kida's return. They pushed up through the ground and rose to encircle Kida in midair. They whirled around her, faster and faster. Beams of light shot from her body.

One by one, the beams of light fell on the Stone Giants that lay throughout the city. The guardians rose like people waking from a long sleep. They formed a ring around Atlantis.

Then, as they clapped their stone hands, a protective dome of energy covered the city—just as the huge wave of lava broke.

The lava flowed harmlessly up the sides of the dome. Milo had saved Kida and Atlantis!

The lava cooled, cracked, and
fell away. Above the plaza, Kida's
glow faded. Her crystalline form dissolved, and she
turned back into the Atlantean princess Milo knew.
Her destiny fulfilled, Kida floated gently down into
Milo's arms.

"Milo," she said weakly. Milo just smiled and held her tightly as the steam cleared to reveal a beautiful new Atlantis—the Atlantis of the past . . . and of their future together.

THE Tigger MOVIE

FAMILY OF TIGGERS

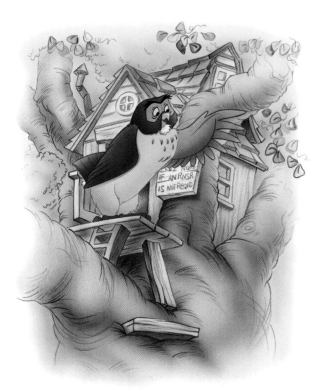

fternoon sunlight lit up the Hundred-Acre Wood. Owl had invited Tigger and Roo for afternoon tea in his tree house.

"Hoo-hoo-HOO!"

cheered Tigger. "You betcha, Beak Lips, me and Roo would love some snappy snacks and drinkedy-drinks!"

"Did I ever tell you the story of how my family first began?" asked Owl.

Owl began to tell Tigger and Roo the story of his family tree.

Meanwhile, Tigger's imagination started to bounce around. A family fulla tiggers, thought Tigger. Now that would be somethin' ta talk about. . . .

"This story goes back a long, long time," Owl went on.

Say, a long, long time ago, thought Tigger, why,

I betcha my family had a saber-toof tigger and a great

big tiggersaurus, too. *R-rr-rowwr-r!*

"And that brings us up to my great-great-grand-mother and my great-great-grandfather," droned Owl. "One day on a morning ride . . ."

Hoo-hoo-*hooo*! thought Tigger. My great-great-grandtigger was probably all fulla vim an' vigor, ridin' along in his little, ol-fashionedy car. I can just see it now. Great-great-grandmomma Tigger sped right past 'im! He was bein' all debonairy, while she was speedin' up an' finishin' up firstest!

Oh, I'm sure and certain my tigger family was terrifically famous for having the most pounce to the ounce! There was a whole buncha athletic tiggers in the Olympics that won great big sporty events like the fifty-yard bounce and the relay pounce.

And there was
a great whole big
buncha gymnastickal
tiggers, too. They
could glide fearlessly
through the air on a
dare without a care.
There was nothin'
more thrillin' than
a tigger tightrope-
walkin'.

And hula-hoopin' tiggerettes. They could whirl up a whoppin' wind with just a few twirls!

And ticklish tiggers that loved to giggle. Hoo-hoo-ha! They sure knew how to have lotsa fun!

There were adventuresome tiggers, like mountain bouncers and deep-sea pouncers. No mountain was too high or ocean too deep that could keep those tiggers away.

And brave captain tiggers that sailed the several seas. With nerves of steel, they weathered through storms on an even keel, makin' new discoveries that made history!

And the chef tiggers cooked up the most

splendiferous sandywiches—on account of their secret

ingredient being real sand, o' course. Hmmm, what

could be more yummy?

And those poetickal tiggers were smart and intelligentickal. They could whip up a rhyme before you could say tiggertime.

Maybe they were the first-ever inventors of the doohickey, the thingamabob, and the whatchamacallit!

And even up in the stars, there were asternaut tiggers and oogly-boogly green Martian tiggers! They scooted those stars into the shape of the Big Tigger and the Little Tigger.

And when I think of those smarty-pants tiggers—
hoo-hoo—they were champion spellers:

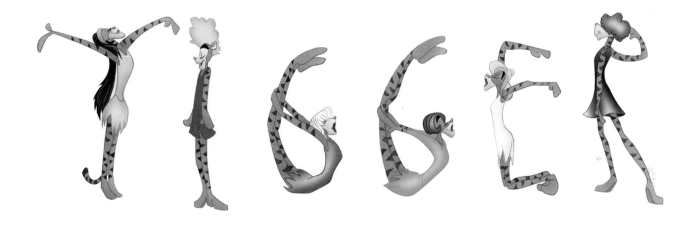

T-I-double-Guh-Rrr spells Tigger! There wasn't a one
who couldn't compete in a spellin' bee.

And, o' course, a tigger never brags, but when it comes to snapping a snazzy shot, we tiggers have always been a more 'n fairly photogenical lot.

"Harrrumph!" said Owl rather loudly. Tigger jumped up and saw Owl and Roo staring at him. "You seem to have slipped into a state of unconscionable unawakeness."

"You were snoring, Tigger," Roo whispered.

Oh, well, Tigger thought. I may have been dreaming about my family fulla tiggers, but what an absoposilutely wunnerful buncha fellas and fellerettes they were! Hoo-hoo-*HOOOOO!*

WALT DISNEY
PICTURES PRESENTS

DINOSAUR

ALADAR'S STORY

I don't know who my parents were or where I came from, but in my memory Lemur Island had always been my home. I was the only dinosaur there.

The lemur clan became my family: Plio; her father, Yar; her daughter, Suri; and my best friend, Zini. Life on Lemur Island was good.

One night, everything changed. An enormous
Fireball fell out of the sky and started rolling toward us!

We leaped into the sea, just as a wave of fire
engulfed the whole island.

We swam to the mainland
and looked back. Our home
was destroyed.

On the mainland, the watering holes had dried up, and there was nothing to eat—except us! A pack of hungry raptors thought we looked like a good meal! The raptors were attacking, when suddenly the ground beneath us began to rumble.

Out of a cloud of
dust, a herd of huge
creatures stomped
toward us, and the raptors fled.

"STAY OUT OF MY WAY!" cried Kron, their leader.

"Look at all the Aladars!" gasped Suri.

As the Herd passed, an even bigger dinosaur, named Baylene, stopped and stared at the lemurs clinging to my back.

"What an unfortunate blemish," she said.

"A good mud bath will clear those right up," added another dinosaur named Eema.

"Um … they're my family," I said. "And my name's Aladar."

"Did I hear you say you were heading for your Nesting Grounds?" asked Plio.

"It's where the Herd goes to have their babies," explained Eema.

But Baylene and Eema were having trouble keeping up with the Herd.

When Kron lumbered past us, I asked, "Maybe you could slow it down a bit?"

Kron sneered at me. His sister, Neera, looked at me as if I were crazy.

These creatures who looked like me were a tough bunch, but the raptors were lurking on the horizon. It was safer to stay with the Herd.

We trudged on through the desert. Then, Eema called out, "The lake! It's just over that hill!"

But when we crested the hill, we saw that the Fireball had dried up the lake, too.

"The Nesting Grounds are only a few days away!" shouted Kron. "Keep moving!"

Then, as Baylene walked across the lake bed, I heard a *squish, squish, squish.*

"Baylene, press down!" I said excitedly. Her footprint began filling with water from underground! Water!

"Look! He found water," Neera said to her brother. I think she was impressed.

That evening, Neera asked me, "Why did you help those old ones?"

"If we look out for one another," I explained, "we all stand a better chance of getting to your Nesting Grounds."

Neera smiled at me.

Suddenly, we heard a terrifying roar. Carnotaurs!

They were deadlier than raptors.

"Move the Herd out!" cried Kron.

A small group of us was left behind.

But we soon found a cave to rest in.

Then, in the middle

of the night, I woke

up. The carnotaurs

stood at the cave

entrance!

We fled deeper into the cave and hoped for a way out.

Before long, Zini asked, "Do you smell that?" He had found fresh air!

I could see a ray of sunlight coming from a small hole!

Baylene pushed on the rocks with all her might. My friends and I joined her. We pushed and pushed as hard as we could.

Craaack! Finally, the wall came tumbling down.

When the dust cleared, we could see before us a lush green valley.

"The Nesting Grounds!" cried Eema.

Next to Lemur Island, it was the most beautiful place I'd ever seen. But . . .

"Where's the Herd?" I asked Eema.

"That is the way we used to get in here," said Eema, looking at a blockaded canyon. Neera and the others were trapped on the other side of a landslide!

As I raced back out of the cave, I spotted another carnotaur. I sneaked away, hurrying to find the Herd.

I found them at the mouth of the blocked canyon. Kron was trying to drive them up the rocky landslide.

"A carnotaur is coming!" I shouted. "I know a new way to the valley. Follow me!"

"They're staying with me," growled Kron. He lunged at me and knocked me down!

Neera rushed to my rescue. With her help, we drove Kron away. Soon, though, we faced an even bigger obstacle: a charging carnotaur!

I wondered if the Herd would run away and try to follow Kron.

"Stand together!" I cried.

The Herd stood firm! They let out the loudest, fiercest bellow I had ever heard. The carnotaur backed off. And, together, we defeated him.

I led the Herd through the cave and into the valley. We got there just in time for nesting.

Everyone helped Neera and me make a nest of our own.

Our valley rang with the happy sounds of families coaxing their babies into the world. Life after the Fireball was not going to be easy, but we had learned that we could do anything if we worked together!

An Icy Adventure

Princess Melody did not know that her mother, Ariel, had once been a mermaid. Melody was just a baby when her parents took her out to sea to meet her grandfather, King Triton, ruler of Atlantica. King Triton had a gift for Melody: a locket that held images

of life under the sea, to remind her of the merpeople.

Suddenly, a crazy sea witch named Morgana showed up and tried to kidnap Melody!

King Triton drove Morgana away with his powerful trident, but, nonetheless, Ariel decided she would have to keep Melody away from the sea for her own safety.

Sadly, King Triton dropped the locket, letting it sink to the ocean floor.

As Melody grew older, her parents did not tell her about Atlantica. And Melody was forbidden to swim

beyond the seawall that surrounded the castle. Melody hated that rule! She loved the

sea and felt at home in the water. Sometimes she would

sneak through the seawall to swim and play in the open

ocean.

One day, Melody found a locket on the ocean floor.

When she brought it home and opened it, a beautiful

vision of a magical

land of mermaids

appeared! But then

Ariel saw the locket

and snapped it shut.

It was the gift King

Triton had wanted to

give Melody years ago, but Ariel could not tell her that.

She feared that Melody would be drawn to the sea and

put herself within Morgana's reach.

Feeling angry and hurt, Melody grabbed the locket

and ran out of the castle. Then she sneaked through the seawall and rowed out to sea in a boat. If her mother would not tell her what the locket meant, Melody would find out on her own.

Morgana's shark, Undertow, was watching Melody.

"Morgana's the best," he told her. "She'll help you." The

young princess was fascinated. Morgana's manta rays

pulled Melody's boat far out to the sea witch's hideout

in an iceberg.

Morgana knew what Melody wanted to hear. "Deep down, you know you weren't meant to be a lowly human," said Morgana. "What you are is something far more enchanting. . . ."

Melody couldn't believe it. "A mermaid?" she

asked hopefully.

Then, with a drop of potion, Morgana turned Melody's legs into mermaid's fins. It was like a dream!

Melody never wanted to be human again, but Morgana warned her that the potion would wear off.

"I could make the spell last longer if I had my magic trident," the witch lied. "Oh, but it was stolen years ago. . . ."

The sea witch was trying to convince Melody to steal King Triton's trident!

Little did Melody know that King Triton was her grandfather—and that the trident rightfully belonged to him, not Morgana. With the trident, Morgana would be ruler of the seas, and she could make the king and all sea creatures bow to her.

Melody fell for the trick. Soon the little mermaid was swimming toward Atlantica. On a nearby iceberg, she asked a penguin and a walrus—Tip and Dash—to help her find the way. "She's a damsel in distress!" said Dash. Diving into the water, the two would-be heroes led Melody to King Triton's palace.

Once there, she hid under a table, watching King Triton. "He doesn't look like a thief," Melody whispered. Still, with Tip and Dash's help, she took the trident when no one was looking.

Melody swam back to Morgana's hideout. Tip and Dash were at her side—until they caught sight of Undertow and swam off in fright. Melody was just about to hand the trident to Morgana when, suddenly, Ariel appeared—as a mermaid! Ariel's old pal, Flounder, was with her.

"Mom!" Melody cried out in surprise. "You're a mermaid?" Ariel tried to explain, but her daughter felt betrayed. "You knew how much I loved the sea," Melody said. "Why did you keep the truth from me?"

Melody still had no idea how evil Morgana was, or how hard her mother had tried to protect Melody from her.

"Please give the trident to me, Melody," Ariel said, pleading.

But it was no use. Melody gave the trident to Morgana, and the sea witch cackled with evil laughter.

She grabbed Ariel with one tentacle, then sealed

Melody and Flounder inside an ice cave. "Your mommy

was only trying to protect you from me," Morgana said.

Melody realized, too late, that she had been tricked!

As the sea witch rose to the water's surface, her spell over Melody wore off. Melody's fins turned back into legs, and she could not breathe underwater anymore. She was trapped below the surface in the ice cave!

Luckily, Tip and Dash returned just in time, rammed the ice wall, and freed Melody.

On an iceberg, Melody watched as Ariel and King Triton were forced to bow to Morgana under the power of the trident.

But the trident had no effect on Melody—she was human!

Quickly, Melody crept up to the top of a huge ice structure and surprised Morgana. They struggled over the trident.

Finally, Melody snatched it away and threw it to King Triton.

"Grandfather!" she cried out. "I believe this belongs to you!"

King Triton blasted Morgana with the trident,

sealing her forever in a block of ice. Melody was reunited with her family, and she hugged her grandfather for the first time.

As a gift to Melody, King Triton gave her a choice:

she could stay with him in Atlantica, or she could

return to her home on land. But Melody had a better

idea. She took the trident and zapped away the seawall

that surrounded the castle. Now the entire family —

merpeople and humans — could finally be together.

TOY STORY 2

BUZZ'S STORY

I could see trouble coming. Andy was playing with me and Woody when . . . *rip!* He tore Woody's arm.

As a Buzz Lightyear action figure, I can take a lot more wear and tear than a pull-string cowboy. So instead of going to Cowboy Camp with Andy, Woody ended up on a dusty shelf.

The next morning, Woody rescued Wheezy, a toy penguin, from being sold in a yard sale by strapping the penguin onto Buster, Andy's dog. But when Buster ran back to the house, Woody fell off. A scoundrel grabbed Woody and sped off with him in his car.

Luckily, I got the license plate: LZTYBRN. Back in Andy's room with the other toys, we decoded the license plate letters with Mr. Spell's help. Soon we had our answer: "Al's Toy Barn!"

Etch A Sketch drew a map to the store. We had to rescue Woody! Rex, Slinky, Hamm, and Mr. Potato Head joined me on the rescue mission.

"Let's move out!" I cried.

By early morning, we reached our destination. But four lanes of zooming traffic stood between us and the store!

Spotting some orange traffic cones nearby, I had an idea. With each of us under a cone, I led the troops safely across.

Once inside the store, I divided up the search team.

Soon I discovered another Buzz Lightyear!

"Space Rangers are to be in hyper-sleep until awakened by authorized personnel!" cried New Buzz.

"You're breaking ranks."

Before I knew it, he

had twist-tied *me* into a box!

Then the troops pulled up in a toy car. Rex had found a *Defeat Zurg* manual for the Buzz Lightyear video game. "You know, Buzz, they make it so you can't defeat Zurg unless you buy this book!" Rex said.

Rex didn't know he was talking to the wrong Buzz! New Buzz hopped into the car, and off they went to find Al—and hopefully Woody!

More determined than ever, I tore myself out of the box. I could see Al leaving the store. New Buzz and the troops had secretly slipped into his bag. I was at Al's heels when —*slam!*—the automatic door shut in my face. I had to knock over dozens of toy boxes to get the door open. Once I got outside, I saw Al heading toward his apartment.

Finally I got into Al's apartment. The troops were
there with New Buzz. And best of all, so was Woody!

"I belong to Andy. I'm the real Buzz," I announced

as I lifted my boot so everyone
could see the word "ANDY"
printed on the bottom. The
troops cheered!

But then Woody told us he wasn't coming home. "I'm a rare Sheriff Woody doll, and these guys are my Roundup Gang," he said. Woody introduced us to Bullseye the horse, Jessie the cowgirl, and the Prospector. Al was going to take them to live in a museum.

"You . . . are . . . a . . . toy!" I shouted at Woody. "You're not a collector's item!"

But Woody just shrugged as if he didn't care about being stuck in some museum!

"Let's go," I told the troops. We headed for the air vent. I couldn't believe Woody wasn't coming home. Then I heard Woody call out, "Buzz!" He had changed his mind!

Woody, Jessie, and Bullseye wanted
to come with us, but the Prospector locked
the air vent—the only way to get out! He
wanted them all to go to the museum.

I had just broken open the vent when Al

came in and packed Woody

and the others in a green

case. I called the troops,

and we raced through the vent

toward the elevator shaft.

At the shaft, we saw a dark figure with gleaming eyes. It was Zurg! He had followed us from the toy store! Zurg attacked. New Buzz began to fight.

"Oh, I can't watch!" Rex said, turning quickly. With a thwack, his tail knocked Zurg off the roof of the elevator. Rex had defeated Zurg!

Inside the elevator, we saw the case with Al beside it. We formed a long

chain with Slinky at the

bottom. Stretching his coils, Slinky unlatched the case.

But before he could grab Woody, the Prospector yanked

him out of reach!

When the elevator stopped, Al stepped out. Before

we knew it, he had driven away in his car.

New Buzz stayed behind while the troops and I
jumped into a Pizza Planet truck parked nearby. We
manned the controls of the truck and followed Al to the
airport. At the terminal, Al rushed through the crowds.

The troops and I climbed into an empty pet carrier

and chased after Al's bags. A conveyor belt took us to

the luggage area. We split up and started looking.

At last, I spotted a green case. I opened it, and out

popped one angry Prospector!

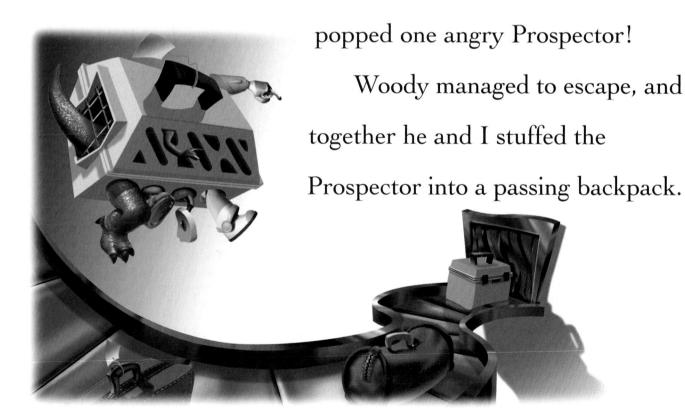

Woody managed to escape, and

together he and I stuffed the

Prospector into a passing backpack.

Bullseye also had freed himself, but Jessie was still trapped inside the green case. Woody and I jumped onto Bullseye's back. Then Woody hopped onto the baggage train that was carrying Jessie away.

Jessie and Woody were loaded onto the plane. Takeoff had begun! I rode Bullseye alongside the plane and saw Jessie and Woody escaping through the landing gear.

Then they jumped— right down to us!

At last, it was time

to go home.

That evening, Andy returned from camp. He ran up to his room. There he spotted Bullseye and Jessie. "Oh, wow! Thanks, Mom!" he cried.

It sure felt great to have Woody back home safe and sound. And it felt great to be one of Andy's toys!

CROSS-COUNTRY CHAOS

Uh-oh. Now Max had done it. Forced to break his first date with Roxanne after his dad, Goofy, planned a father-son road trip, Max had fibbed. He told Roxanne that his dad was driving him to the televised Powerline rock concert in Los Angeles. He even lied and said that Goofy was friends with Powerline. Then Max promised to wave to Roxanne on TV.

Roxanne was so impressed, she wasn't mad that Max had broken their date. But now Max was miserable. Miles from home, with no chance of fulfilling his promise, Max took out his frustration on his dad. "This is the stupidest vacation!" he yelled.

Since Max was barely speaking to him, poor Goofy had no idea what was going on.

Then, at a campground, they bumped into Goofy's boss, Pete, and his son, PJ. On the roof deck of Pete's deluxe RV, Pete gave Goofy a parenting tip on keeping teenagers out of trouble: be firm.

So Goofy decided to *make* Max have a good time. "Get your gear. We're goin' fishin'!" he ordered, and grabbed his pole.

Down at the lake, Goofy demonstrated "the perfect cast," accidentally hooking Pete's steak on the end of the fishing line and sending it flying clear across the water.

"And now we reel it in," Goofy said to Max. It was a big one, all right! Goofy pulled and strained and reeled in a . . . Bigfoot! Goofy and Max took off. They made it to their car just in time.

But where were the keys? Outside the car, Bigfoot
jingled the key ring. They were trapped. Now Max *had*
to talk to his dad. Over a can of soup that they warmed
by using the cigarette lighter, Goofy reminded Max
that the two of them had once been very close.

Max felt bad. He
knew he was being
difficult. But he didn't
think his dad would
understand.

Late that night,
as Bigfoot snoozed on top of their car and Goofy
snored in the driver's seat, Max did something
desperate. On the road map, he erased the route
Goofy had marked and plotted a new course . . . for
Los Angeles.

Back on the road the next day, Max felt awful about what he had done. And to make matters worse, Goofy had made him the official trip navigator.

"I trust ya wholeheartedly, son," Goofy said. Max did not know what to say, so he didn't say anything.

A few nights later at a motel, Goofy and Max met up again with Pete and PJ. Before long, Pete got wind of what Max was up to and informed Goofy: "I heard the little mutant telling PJ that he changed the map, so you're headin' straight to L.A., pal."

Goofy was crushed. He did not want to believe that Max would lie to him. But after a few

more miles on the road, it was clear: they were headed due west to L.A.

Furious, Goofy pulled the car off the road and climbed out. Max followed, trying to explain. But just then, the car started rolling down the canyon road!

Goofy and Max raced after the runaway car and reached it just before it splashed into the river below. Then, as they floated downstream, Max finally told his dad everything: about Roxanne, about the lie, and about how he had changed their route.

Instead of scolding him, Goofy said, "Well, I think

 the only thing for us to do now is to get you up onstage with this Powerline feller!"

Just then Max realized something was terribly

wrong. They were headed right for a waterfall! Goofy

managed to get

ashore, where

he used his

fishing pole

to cast a line

toward Max.

The hook caught hold of the car as it was rolling over

the falls, but then —*crack!*— the log Goofy was standing

on snapped. He fell into the river.

Meanwhile, all of their gear from the car had spilled out into the water. Backpacks and sleeping bags floated here and there. Max got tangled up in their tent. As he went over the falls, the tent deployed into a makeshift parachute. Max was saved! Then, after getting a hold of the fishing pole, Max cast a line toward Goofy—and reeled him in!

"Boy, what a crazy vacation!" exclaimed Max.

"And it's not over yet!" replied Goofy. Together they hatched a plan. Before Max knew it,

he and his dad were in L.A., climbing out of instrument cases backstage at the Powerline concert. Their scheme had worked! Now they just had to get onstage. The concert was starting!

But Max and Goofy got separated. Max ran from a security guard, while Goofy stumbled inside a large stage prop. When the prop was transported onstage, Goofy popped out.

Then, swinging on a lighting cable to evade the guard, Max joined him.

Max couldn't believe it! He and his dad were onstage and on TV— dancing with Powerline!

Back at home, Max's first stop was Roxanne's house. Even though he had got onstage with

Powerline, he had to tell Roxanne that he had lied.

"I guess I just wanted you to like me," he explained to her.

"I already liked you, Max," Roxanne replied.

Then she asked Max if he was free that evening.

"How 'bout tomorrow?" he said. That night, Max

had plans . . . with his dad!

THE SORCERER'S APPRENTICE

Long ago in a long-lost land there lived a man of magic. He was known far and wide as the Sorcerer. All the powers of the world were at his command: fire, water, wind, and earth. There was nothing he could not do.

One day, a young lad named Mickey appeared at the door and begged to be taken on as the Sorcerer's apprentice.

"I have no time to teach you tricks," the Sorcerer muttered as he searched impatiently for his magic hat.

The Sorcerer was about to send him away when Mickey whisked a red silk scarf off a table. Beneath it was the Sorcerer's magic hat. "Is this what you are

looking for?" Mickey asked.

At that, the Sorcerer realized that perhaps he could use a bright young apprentice.

Mickey soon set to work sweeping and swabbing. Sometimes he would sneak away from his chores and secretly watch the Sorcerer at work. How he longed to be like the old man with his vast knowledge of spells!

Late one night, the Sorcerer removed his magic hat

and placed it on

the table. Then,

as he went

upstairs, he

asked Mickey

to do one last

chore and fill

the vat with

water before he

went to bed.

As soon as the Sorcerer was out of sight, Mickey picked up the magic hat and put it on just to see how it fit. Suddenly, Mickey felt a strange surge

and knew that now he had magical powers, too.

Spotting his old broom, the Sorcerer's apprentice took a deep breath and began to chant: *"Dooma, dooma, brooma, brooma . . ."*

Magically, the broom came to life, sprouting two arms of its own.

Mickey motioned for the enchanted broom to pick up two buckets and follow him to the fountain in the courtyard. There he directed the broom to fill the two buckets with water and carry them back to the

vat. Since the vat was quite large, Mickey had the broom continue to fetch more water.

Quite pleased with himself, Mickey settled back in the Sorcerer's big chair to enjoy a few minutes' rest. He soon fell asleep to the soothing sound of water splashing into the vat. . . .

In his dream, Mickey slowly ascended to the top of a pinnacle. Above him was a starry sky; below, a silken sea. With a flutter of his fingers, Mickey made the stars circle around his head like a crown of fire. Then he leaned over the water and drew the tides to him.

The waves were lapping at his feet. . . .

Mickey awoke with a start, waist high in water. The broom was still filling the vat with water! He watched in horror as the water came cascading over the rim!

"Stop!"
Mickey cried.
"Halt!" But the
broom neither
heard nor heeded.
In desperation,
Mickey picked up
an ax and broke
the enchanted
broom into
many pieces.

Mickey left the room and shut the door. But just then each of the broom splinters began to come alive! Soon there was an army of marching brooms—each with two buckets. Mickey heard the noise and opened the door a crack to peek outside. A parade of brooms trampled right over him!

As the brooms steadily poured more and more water into the vat, Mickey frantically bailed the water out a nearby window. But it was no use. For every bucket he managed to bail out, each of the brooms poured in two more.

Whirling and swirling, the water swept Mickey
off his feet and carried him away. Then the Sorcerer's

book drifted by.

Mickey scrambled

aboard the big

book as if it were

a life raft and

frantically started

searching for a

spell to undo

the damage.

Suddenly, a beam of white light pierced the darkness. Mickey looked up, and there, on the stairs, stood his master.

Slowly, the Sorcerer raised his arms. He murmured some words, thrust both arms straight out, and pointed his fingers at the terrible torrent.

Instantly, the raging sea parted, and the waters began to recede. And when the last swirl of water had vanished, there Mickey stood, wet and shivering, in a shallow puddle.

As Mickey gazed up sheepishly, the Sorcerer stared down at him with cold, angry eyes. Mickey took off the magic hat and returned it to its owner. Then, with downcast eyes, he rushed off to complete his chores.

And so Mickey never even saw the sly little smile the Sorcerer flashed as he picked up the once enchanted broom. But from then on, the Sorcerer found a few minutes each day to teach his pupil the true uses of magic.

DISNEY·PIXAR

MONSTERS, INC.

THE BIG BOO RESCUE

Sulley was the top Scarer at Monsters, Inc., the biggest energy supply company in Monstropolis. But at the moment, being number one didn't matter much

at all. Sulley had to save Boo, the human child he had accidentally let into the monster world!

In a secret lab at Monsters, Inc., Boo was being held prisoner. A vacuumlike scream machine—built to extract powerful screams from human children—hung over her head. Randall Boggs, another Scarer at Monsters, Inc., and the company president, Mr. Waternoose, were about to use poor Boo to get unlimited scream energy!

Just in time, Sulley burst into the lab. He knocked

the machine
away from Boo
and freed her
from the chair
she was in.

"Kitty!"
Boo exclaimed
in relief as
Sulley picked
her up.

Before Sulley could escape with Boo, Randall

attacked him. Sulley was struggling with Randall when

Sulley's best friend,

Mike, arrived and

helped Sulley and

Boo get away. The

chase was on!

Sulley, Mike, and

Boo ran down the

hall, with Randall

close behind.

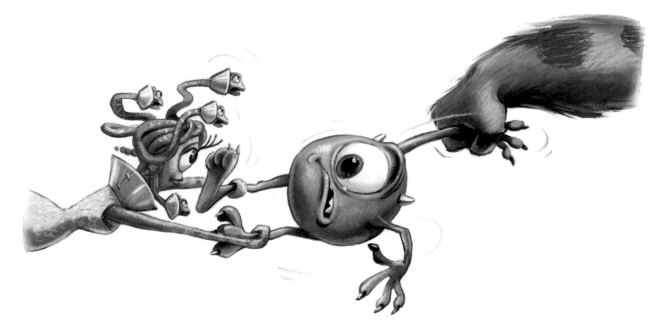

Mike glanced over his shoulder and saw his girlfriend, Celia, her snake hair angrily hissing at him. She tried to stop him so he would tell her what was going on. Mike explained that there was a human child in Monstropolis and that Waternoose and Randall were after them.

Suddenly, Celia realized how she could help Mike and Sulley. "Attention, employees. Randall Boggs has just broken the all-time scare record!" she fibbed over the loudspeaker.

A mob of monsters crowded around Randall to congratulate him.

"Get out of my way!" Randall yelled.

Meanwhile, Sulley, Mike, and Boo had reached the Scare Floor, where children's doors were delivered so monsters could go into their rooms and scare them. They grabbed onto a passing door and were whisked away

into the giant door vault of Monsters, Inc.

Rows of children's closet doors were spread out before them. Boo's door was just ahead. If they could get to Boo's door and get Boo through it, she would be back at home, safe and sound.

But Randall was still after them, climbing from door to door and getting closer!

Just then, Sulley, Mike, and Boo came to a door sorter. It sent Boo's door one way while they went another—and hit a dead end. What would they do now?

"Make Boo laugh," Sulley told Mike. They knew that a child's laughter contained even more energy than a child's scream.

Mike bonked himself on the head. Boo laughed, and all the doors powered up!

Now, Sulley, Mike, and Boo had a new way to lose Randall. They could use one door to enter a room in the human world, then reenter the vault through a different door.

Sulley, Mike, and Boo went through the door they'd been riding. That door landed them in a beach house in Hawaii. Another door dropped them in Japan. But Randall was always just a step or two behind them.

Sulley and Mike opened a door, and they all jumped into a room. Randall ran through the door, but he couldn't find them. After Randall passed by, Sulley and Mike dropped from the ceiling. Then they raced back the way they'd come. Randall was right behind them.

Randall launched himself at the open door. And —*smack!*— the door slammed right in his face.

Behind the closed door, Mike chuckled. "I hope that hurt!" he said.

But Randall wasn't down for long.

Just when Sulley thought they were safe, Randall appeared out of nowhere. He pounced on the door that Sulley and Mike were riding and plucked Boo out of Sulley's arms!

Then Randall pulled out the pin that held the door to the track. Mike and Sulley, still clinging to the door, dropped into the depths of the vault. Luckily, Mike managed to wrench open the door. He and Sulley crawled inside and shut the door seconds before it crashed to the ground.

High up in the vault, another door opened. Sulley peeked out. He spotted Boo and Randall riding a door far below. Sulley leaped from door to door, heading toward them.

Randall opened the door and darted inside. Sulley followed.

The first thing Sulley noticed was Boo standing safe and sound on the other side of the room. "Boo!" he cried in relief. But just then Randall sprang down on him, knocking him back out the open door!

As he fell
into the door
vault, Sulley
desperately
reached out and
caught the edge of
the door.

Randall
bent down and began to
pry Sulley's fingers from the door.

Suddenly, Randall screamed in pain. Boo was yanking on his head!

Sulley jumped back into the room and grabbed Randall. "You did it, Boo! You beat him!" Sulley cried. He pitched Randall through an open door. Mike slammed it shut and dropped the door into the vault. And that was the end of Randall.

Sulley had saved
Boo. And, when
it mattered most,
Boo had
overcome
her fear of
Randall . . .
and saved
Sulley
in return.

GOING TO THE DOGS

After spending three years in prison for stealing ninety-nine Dalmatian puppies, Cruella De Vil was free. She had been able to convince the judge that she now loved dogs. But the judge had one warning for Cruella: if she repeated her crime, he would take away

her freedom *and* her fortune!

As Cruella exited the prison, her ever faithful valet, Alonso, greeted her with a gift—a hairless dog.

"I think I'll call him Fluffy," Cruella announced, delighted.

Across town, Kevin Shepherd ran the Second Chance Dog Shelter. Kevin really loved dogs.

He was playing tug-of-war with a dog named Drooler, while the other dogs and Waddlesworth—a macaw who thought he was a dog—looked on.

But life at Second Chance was not all fun and games. The rent had not been paid, and the landlord was threatening to evict Kevin and the dogs.

"You and your mangy pack are out of here tomorrow!" the landlord shouted.

Kevin didn't know what to do.

The next day, the landlord came back to kick Kevin out. But Cruella heard about the situation and decided to buy the place! She transformed the Second Chance Dog Shelter into a palace. The dogs were even given bubble baths and new hairstyles.

But Chloe Simon, Cruella's probation officer, was not so sure

Cruella was cured. In fact, Cruella had tried to make

Chloe's own dog Dipstick into a fur coat a few years ago!

More

recently,

Chloe's

Dalmatians,

Dottie and

Dipstick,

had become

proud parents of puppies. Their names were Domino,

Little Dipper, and Oddball.

Chloe brought her dogs to work on the same day that Cruella came in for a visit. While Chloe talked to Cruella, one of the puppies got into trouble. Oddball, who didn't have spots yet, saw the copier repairman covered in ink spots. She raced over to get some of her own. But after Oddball rolled around in the ink, the repairman accidentally knocked her out the window!

It was Cruella who first looked out the window and spotted Oddball. She also saw the two other puppies, who had gone out to try to rescue her!

Chloe rushed to the window. One by one, she was able to pull the puppies safely back into the room.

Just then, Big Ben, the famous London clock, began to chime. It had a strange effect on Cruella. Her old dog-hating, fur-loving nature was returning!

Everywhere she looked she saw spots! She ran into the street, shouting, "Cruella's ba-a-a-ck! Ha-ha-ha-ha!"

Cruella ran home and found a design for a hooded Dalmatian puppy coat that she had sketched years ago. Then she sent Alonso out to steal 102 Dalmatian puppies while she went to visit the furrier Jean-Pierre LePelt. Together they plotted to create the spotted coat.

Meanwhile, Chloe and Kevin happened to meet up in the park. They were enjoying a puppet show along

with their pets, when Oddball got entangled in some balloon strings and started floating away. Luckily, Kevin was able

to grab the balloons and rescue Oddball.

Later on, Kevin and Chloe went out on a date. Waddlesworth came along and brought Oddball a spotted sweater.

Chloe liked Kevin, but she couldn't understand why he trusted Cruella. Kevin explained that Cruella had every reason to be good: if she was ever cruel to

an animal again, the judge would give all her money to the Second Chance Animal Shelter!

The next day, the police came to Kevin's shelter, looking for stolen Dalmatian puppies. They searched and found a sackful of puppies. Then Chloe and Cruella

arrived. Cruella accused Kevin of setting her up to get her money. But, in fact, Cruella had set Kevin up! She wanted to make sure someone else took the blame for her crime. Kevin and his pets were taken to jail!

That evening, Cruella invited Chloe and Dipstick to a fancy party at her mansion. Cruella welcomed them and asked, "Are your little spotted puppies safe and snug at home?" Little did Chloe know that Cruella had sent LePelt to steal Dipstick and Dottie's puppies!

Then Dipstick heard a tiny bark. Cruella's dog Fluffy was beckoning to him. He and Chloe followed Fluffy to Cruella's fur room. There Chloe discovered the design for the Dalmatian puppy coat. Just then Cruella appeared—and locked Chloe in the room! But Dipstick escaped and raced home.

At Chloe's house, LePelt was struggling to get the dogs into a sack. Oddball sounded the Twilight Bark just before LePelt captured her. Soon dogs all over London were barking the alarm. Dipstick arrived home just as LePelt was driving

off. Bravely, he leaped inside the truck that was carrying his family away.

In prison, Kevin and his pets also heard the Twilight Bark. "We have to get out of here!" Kevin said.

Waddlesworth waddled over to the guard and stole his keys. Then he set Kevin and the others free!

Back at Cruella's house, Fluffy helped Chloe escape, too.

At the same time, Kevin and Chloe arrived at Chloe's apartment to find the dogs were gone! But Drooler found a clue—a train ticket. Cruella and LePelt would be on the 10 P.M. Orient Express to Paris! Kevin, Chloe, and the pets raced across town to the train station.

When they arrived, they saw Oddball racing along-side the departing Orient Express. She had got away from Cruella, but was trying to hop aboard the train to save her family.

Waddlesworth, who never thought he could fly, now realized he *had* to. Flapping his wings furiously, he flew to Oddball, lifted her up, and dropped her safely on the train.

In Paris, Cruella and LePelt drove the puppies to LePelt's workshop where Alonso locked them in the cellar. Oddball and Waddlesworth had been hiding in the backseat, unnoticed. They sneaked into the workshop, and Waddlesworth began tearing at  a hole leading into the cellar. If he could make the hole big enough, all of the puppies could escape!

Meanwhile, through the Twilight Bark, Kevin and Chloe realized the puppies were in LePelt's workshop.

But just as they arrived and opened the cellar door, Cruella came up from behind and locked them inside! They were trapped—but now the hole that Waddlesworth had been working on was large enough for the puppies to crawl through and get away!

Just then, Cruella saw Oddball leading the
puppies up the stairs and out the window! Enraged,
she raced after them across a narrow bridge and into
the bakery next door.

Cruella did her best to get the puppies, but she had no chance against the 102 Dalmatians. In the end, Cruella was baked into a cake—icing and all. The police took Cruella away. The puppies were safe and sound!

Several days later, Alonso arrived at Second Chance Dog Shelter with a check in the amount of Cruella's entire estate. The judge had kept his promise. All of Cruella's money would go to the dogs.

As the celebrating began, Chloe suddenly noticed something. "Oddball's got her spots!" she cried, pointing to the little puppy. No more spotted sweaters for Oddball. She finally had the real thing!

Disney's
The Many Adventures Of
WINNIE
The POOH

THREE FRIENDLY TALES

POOH GETS STUCK

Pooh's nose twitched as he stood outside Rabbit's house. "Hello!" Pooh shouted. "Is anybody home?"

"Is that you, Pooh?" asked a reluctant Rabbit from inside. "Oh dear. It is you. Well, come in, Pooh. I'm just having a little snack of bread and . . . honey. Would you like some honey on your bread?" Rabbit asked after he let Pooh in.

"Never mind about the bread. I'll just take a small helping of honey," said Pooh. And so Pooh began to eat. And he ate and ate and ate . . . until Rabbit had no honey left.

Pooh stood to go. "Thank you, Rabbit," he said. "That was delicious." Then Pooh pushed himself into

the hole that was the doorway to Rabbit's house. But he didn't get far. Instead, he got *stuck*!

"It all comes from eating too much honey!" said Rabbit.

Rabbit ran out his back door and got Christopher Robin. But even Christopher Robin could not unstick poor Pooh.

"Pooh Bear, there's only one thing we can do: wait for you to get thin again," Christopher Robin finally said.

Soon Gopher, the excavation expert, arrived. He knew how to dig, but he didn't know anything about getting bears out of holes.

Gopher opened his lunch box. "Care for some honey?" he asked Pooh.

"Oh no!" cried Rabbit, racing out of his house.

"Don't feed the bear!" Rabbit was getting tired of having part of Pooh in his living room.

Finally, one morning, Pooh budged! Christopher

Robin came back with all of Pooh's friends. Eeyore

pulled on Kanga. Kanga pulled on Christopher Robin.

Christopher Robin pulled on Pooh as hard as he could.

But Pooh was still stuck.

The others were pulling as hard as they could outside Rabbit's house. Inside his house, Rabbit aimed his head and got ready to run. Picking up speed, he smashed into Pooh's backside, pushing with all his might.

Pop! Pooh shot right out of Rabbit's front door and flew up into the sky like a rocket.

"Watch out!" yelled Christopher Robin as Pooh sailed toward a big tree. Pooh's head and shoulders disappeared right into another hole—this one high up in the tree.

"Don't worry, Pooh. We'll get you out!" Christopher Robin cried. But Pooh was not at all unhappy. The hole where he had landed was full of honey!

"No hurry!" Pooh yelled back. "Take your time." Then he laughed and sang as he dipped his paws into the golden honey.

RABBIT GETS LOST

A few weeks later, Rabbit was out picking carrots in his garden. "Halloooo!" called Tigger as he bounced through the garden, upsetting Rabbit's plants.

"Oops. Sorry about that," said Tigger after Rabbit scolded him. "But bouncing's what tiggers do best!"

Early the next morning, Pooh, Piglet, and Tigger met Rabbit in the woods. As usual, Tigger bounced ahead of everybody.

"Listen," whispered Rabbit, "I have a plan. Let's teach Tigger a lesson to scare the bounce out of him. We'll take him deep into the woods and then we'll lose him."

So, deep in the woods, they hid from Tigger in an old tree trunk. Pooh and Piglet worried that Tigger would be scared. But Rabbit

whispered, "We are going to lose Tigger just for tonight. We'll find him again in the morning."

Tigger searched high and low for his friends. Then he bounced off into the woods.

After Tigger had bounced out of sight, the three friends started home. But the woods looked different now.

Pooh asked Rabbit if they were going in circles.

"That's ridiculous!" said Rabbit. "You wait here. I'll walk away, and if I don't come back, that proves we are not going in circles."

After a nap, Pooh and Piglet found their way home easily. Pooh just followed his tummy to his honeypots. But Rabbit was still wandering around, lost in the mist. All around he heard frightening noises.

"Help!" wailed Rabbit. "Piglet! Pooh! Somebody! Oh please help me!"

Suddenly, Tigger came bouncing out of the mist. "Halloo, Rabbit!" he said.

"Tigger!" cried Rabbit. "You're supposed to be lost."

"Tiggers never get lost, bunny boy!" Tigger exclaimed. "Grab my tail. I'll bounce ya outta here." And Tigger bounced a very humble and quiet Rabbit all the way home.

BOUNCE, TIGGER, BOUNCE

That winter, Tigger took Roo out to play. Roo loved Tigger because he was fun and brave.

Roo pointed to a tall tree. "Tigger," he said, "I bet you could climb that tall, tall tree in just five bounces!" And Tigger bounced up the tree, right to the top.

But at the top, Tigger did something tiggers don't often do. He looked down. "Oh no," said Tigger. "I forgot that tiggers don't climb trees." He looked down again. "How did this tree get so high?" Tigger held onto the tree trunk as tightly as he could.

Roo let go of Tigger's tail and landed on a lower branch. Just then, Tigger saw Pooh and Piglet, who had come out to play in the snow. "Halloooo!" Tigger shouted, startling his friends with his booming voice.

"Tigger is stuck!" Roo called down to Pooh and Piglet.

It wasn't long before Christopher Robin and the others heard that Tigger and Roo were in trouble. Christopher Robin took off his winter coat. Pooh, Kanga, and Piglet each grabbed a corner.

"Jump!" Christopher Robin yelled to Roo. "We'll catch you."

"Wheeee!" cried Roo as he jumped. And he landed safely in the warm coat.

Then it was Tigger's turn. But Tigger wouldn't jump. He held on even tighter. "Oh if I ever get out of this, I promise never to bounce again," said Tigger. "Never!"

Rabbit was thrilled by Tigger's promise never to bounce again. He helped Christopher Robin convince Tigger to slide down the tree, one inch at a time.

THE MANY ADVENTURES OF WINNIE THE POOH

It took a long time, but Tigger finally got down. "I'm so happy, I feel like bouncing!" cried Tigger as soon as he reached the ground.

"Ah-ah-ah." Rabbit shook his head. "You promised never to bounce again."

Tigger remembered. But he looked so sad that everyone—including Rabbit—felt sorry for him.

"Well, I—ah . . . oh all right!" Rabbit finally said. "Tigger can have his bounce back."

"Hoo-hoo-hoo! Thank you, Rabbit!" Tigger cried. "Come on! Let's all bounce!"

And so, Pooh and all his friends bounced off into the snowy Hundred-Acre Wood, where they shared many more wonderful adventures.

Walt Disney's
Chip 'n' Dale

A Nutty Visit to the Zoo

Chip 'n' Dale, two little chipmunks, were having a busy day. They were gathering nuts for their winter's food. One by one, Dale tossed the nuts up to Chip in their tree. And Chip swiftly stored each away.

Toss, catch, toss, catch; they had been at work all day.

Suddenly, Dale cried, "Look at this one!" And he

threw up yet another nut. Chip took a look at the nut

that sailed up. It was long and strangely shaped.

"Open it," said Dale, scrambling up the tree. So Chip snapped it open; the shell was paper-thin. Inside was not one nut, but two!

"Let's try them," said Chip. So they each ate one. And how good those peanuts did taste!

"Let's find some more of these," said Dale.

"Okay," said Chip. So away

they went, racing up and down their tree and other trees nearby. They searched high and low for more peanuts, but they couldn't find a single one.

Then Chip 'n' Dale climbed up a high brick wall that stood near their tree. Beyond the wall was a zoo. There were lots of big animals behind fences. And outside the fences were people tossing peanuts to the animals!

"Look at that!" cried Chip.

"Let's go!" said Dale.

But where should they go first? The monkeys looked too lively. They caught every peanut that was thrown to them. The bears looked too brawny, and rather fierce. And no one threw any peanuts to the camels or lions or tigers, which was probably just as well.

"How about this?" asked Dale when they came to the seals' pool. The seals looked friendly, sitting on their rocks. And they were clapping their flippers as if they had just had a treat.

"I'll try it," said Chip. So he scrambled up onto the rocks beside the seals.

But instead of tossing crispy peanuts, the zookeeper threw him a fish!

That was enough of the seals for Chip 'n' Dale!

They wandered on, feeling rather sad.

Then they came to the elephant.

The elephant stood there, big and slow, in what seemed like a sea of peanuts.

"This is for us!" said Chip to Dale. So in through the fence they climbed.

They scooped up whole big armloads of peanuts. Then, ever so quietly, they started for the wall that stood between the zoo and their hollow tree. Dale tossed his armload of peanuts into what he thought was the doorway in their tree.

"Why, that's the elephant's mouth!" cried Chip.

"Mouth!" cried Dale, and he ran away so fast that he bumped into Chip at top speed—and scattered Chip's peanuts everywhere.

They were not ready to give up, though. They waited in the shadows until the elephant was busy again. Then they filled their arms once more and started for the wall again.

They made it to the top of the high brick wall with their armloads safe and sound.

Then—*rat-a-tat-tat!*—they were pelted with nuts from behind. The elephant had spotted them at the last minute and was shooting peanuts at them from his trunk!

Poor Chip 'n' Dale dropped their loads and ran.
They hid behind some tree branches until all was quiet again.

Then, feeling sore all over, they crept back home.

"I guess we can get along without peanuts," said Chip sadly.

So, back to
work they went
on their own
store of nuts,
Dale tossing
them one by
one from below,
Chip catching them
up above. But they were so
tired now that the work seemed very slow.

"Let's take a little rest," said Chip.

It was while they were resting that they heard a sound like the patter of rain on leaves. But it wasn't rain, for the sun was shining.

The elephant was peeking over the wall. He felt sorry for Chip 'n' Dale. So with the zookeeper on his head to help aim, the elephant was squirting a year's supply of peanuts into Chip 'n' Dale's hollow tree!

And ever since, those chipmunks Chip 'n' Dale and the elephant in the zoo have been the very best of friends! Just think of that!

WALT DISNEY
PICTURES PRESENTS

Lady and the Tramp II
SCAMP'S ADVENTURE

ONE OF THE PACK

Rules, rules, rules. Scamp hated rules. Lady and Tramp's other puppies were obedient and good. But Scamp liked to play. And sometimes, when Scamp played, he forgot about the rules. He tracked mud into the house and chewed on Jim Dear's hats.

So one
night, Jim
Dear decided
that Scamp
had to sleep
outside,
chained to

the doghouse. Tramp tried to explain to his son that

being part of a family meant following certain rules.

"But I want to run wild and free—like a real dog!"

Scamp replied.

Later, Scamp heard dogs howling on the other side of the fence. He peeked through the gate and watched as a group of street dogs outwitted a dogcatcher. They were so wild! Scamp wanted to join them, but his chain held him back. The dogs ran off.

Then, as Scamp dreamed about life without fences or leashes, it happened. He pulled against the chain, and it broke loose from his collar! Scamp was free!

"Hey, you guys!" Scamp shouted after the street dogs. "Wait for me!"

Scamp ran through the dark streets, looking for the dogs. He caught up with one of them, Angel, in a dark alley. "Listen," Angel said to Scamp, "you don't belong on the street."

Scamp wouldn't listen. He followed Angel to the junkyard, the dogs' hangout. There he met Buster, the rough and tough leader of the Junkyard Dogs. Buster agreed to let Scamp be one of them . . . if Scamp could pass a test of courage.

It wouldn't be easy. Scamp had to fetch a can

from the paws of a sleeping dog—a mean, vicious dog

named Reggie. Scamp managed to slide the can free

and was tiptoeing away when—*clang!*—he ran right

into a garbage can. Reggie awoke with a snarl.

In a flash, Reggie was after Scamp. Somehow, Angel accidentally wound up in the middle of the chase. She fled around a corner—and right into the path of the dogcatcher's truck. The dogcatcher scooped Angel up in his net.

Scamp had to save her! He leaped and grabbed onto the long handle of the net with his teeth. The truck swerved. Reggie ran out into the road and *crash!* The truck knocked Reggie into a fruit stand. The dogcatcher nabbed Reggie, but Scamp and Angel got away.

Scamp got the can *and* saved Angel! But Buster still wasn't convinced that Scamp was ready to be a Junkyard Dog. He still had one more test for Scamp.

Then, Scamp and Angel went for a stroll around town. They chased fireflies. They shared a plate of spaghetti outside Tony's restaurant. It was a real case of puppy love.

Later, while chasing a squirrel, Scamp and Angel ended up on Jim Dear and Darling's street. Jim Dear was out with Tramp and Lady, looking for Scamp. Scamp and Angel hid as they went by.

"C'mon, Tramp," Jim Dear was saying. "We'll find Scamp tomorrow." The three went home.

"The Tramp is your father?" Angel whispered to Scamp. She told him that Tramp was a legend among street dogs. Scamp couldn't believe it. His dad had once been a Junkyard Dog?

Scamp and Angel crept up to the house and peeked through the window. Scamp was surprised by how sad his family looked. He didn't think they'd miss him so much.

"I can't believe you'd run away from a home like this!" Angel said to him. She desperately wanted a family of her own. But Scamp still wanted to be wild and free. One more test to pass—and he'd be a Junkyard Dog.

That test came the next day at the big Fourth of

July picnic. Jim Dear and Darling were there with

Aunt Sarah, Lady, Tramp, and the other pups. Buster

dared Scamp to steal some chicken from his own family's

picnic! Scamp didn't want to, but he did it, anyway.

Tramp chased after Scamp and tried to talk him into coming home. But Scamp said no. Tramp was crushed, but he told his son, "When you've had enough, our door's always open."

Then, since Scamp had passed his final test, Buster took off Scamp's collar. He was now a real Junkyard Dog—wild and free.

But Scamp's freedom did not last very long. That very same night, Buster betrayed him! He set Scamp up to be nabbed by the dogcatcher. "Well, lookee here. No collar," said the dogcatcher. Scamp was going straight to the pound.

Scamp was cold, alone, and afraid. He realized he had turned his back on his own family for a scoundrel like Buster. "I wish I were home," said Scamp to himself.

Luckily, Angel spotted Scamp in the back of the

 dogcatcher's truck. She raced to Jim Dear and Darling's house and found Tramp. "Hurry!" she said. "Scamp's in trouble!"

Meanwhile, at the pound, Scamp was thrown into a cage with . . . Reggie!

Reggie had just grabbed hold of the pup when Tramp burst through the door. With a few old street-dog moves, Tramp rescued Scamp from Reggie *and* the pound.

"I'm so sorry," Scamp said to his dad. "I shouldn't have run away."

Tramp took Scamp and Angel home with him. Scamp's family was so happy to see him . . . and his new friend. "Oh, she's a little Angel!" said Darling. They were one big happy family again—with one very happy new member.

As for Scamp, he still didn't like his baths. But it sure was good to be home.

Walt Disney's

MICKEY MOUSE

BRAVE LITTLE TAILOR

Once upon a time, there was a tailor named Mickey. He lived in a kingdom ruled by a good king and the beautiful Princess Minnie. All was well in the land until a terrible giant appeared. The king offered a rich reward to the one who could get rid of the giant.

"Have you ever killed a giant?" the butcher asked the baker.

Before the baker could answer, Mickey declared, "I killed seven with one blow!"

Now, Mickey was talking about flies, not giants. But he was called before the royal court. And before he could explain that he had killed seven flies, not giants, Mickey was appointed Royal Giant Slayer.

Mickey was sent to work right away. He went out into the country in search of the giant. As it turned out, the giant was not hard to find. What *was* hard was staying out from under the giant's great big feet!

"Yikes!" cried Mickey, leaping into a cart of pumpkins.

"Food!" exclaimed the giant, reaching for the pile of pumpkins.

To the giant, pumpkins were no bigger than grapes. He popped them into his mouth. And he popped Mickey in, too! Oh, no! Mickey was trapped in the giant's mouth!

To wash down his
pumpkin snack, the
giant tore a well right
out of the ground. As
he drank, the water
flowed from the well
into the giant's mouth,

carrying with it the well bucket, still tied to the well.
Thinking quickly, Mickey grabbed hold of the bucket.
When the giant finished his drink and took the well
from his lips, out came the bucket. Mickey was free!

Now the brave little tailor had a plan. Mickey leaped from the bucket onto the giant's arm. Then he slipped under the giant's shirt and crawled up his sleeve.

A giant hand chased Mickey into the sleeve.

Mickey used his tailor's scissors to cut his way out.

When the giant's hand followed him out of this new hole, Mickey went to work and sewed it up again.

The giant's hand was caught in his own sleeve!

Finally, Mickey swung around and around the giant, hanging onto the end of the long length of thread. Within moments, Mickey had the giant all tied up.

When the giant tried to get away, he stumbled and fell. The terrible giant hit his head and passed out. Soon he was snoring soundly. Then Mickey tied the giant up with strong ropes so he couldn't get away.

The brave little tailor had neatly sewn up the giant problem. His reward was one million golden pazoozahs. And, in the eyes of Princess

Minnie, it certainly didn't hurt that the brave little tailor was the kingdom's biggest hero.

Naturally, Mickey and Minnie lived happily ever after.

Disney's THE RETURN of JAFAR

IAGO TO THE RESCUE

All was well in Agrabah. The evil genie Jafar was defeated and imprisoned in his lamp. Aladdin had a new home at the palace with Princess Jasmine and the Sultan. And Genie was back from his trip around the world.

"I got souvenirs for everybody!" exclaimed Genie.

And, to
top it all off,
the Sultan had
made Aladdin
his Royal
Vizier—his

most trusted adviser. Imagine the Sultan's surprise at

Aladdin's first official piece of advice: to allow Jafar's

old sidekick, Iago the parrot, to stay at the palace. Now

that Iago was out from under Jafar's spell, Aladdin

thought he could be trusted.

The Sultan was skeptical, but he agreed—as long as Aladdin kept an eye on Iago.

Meanwhile, out in the desert, a thief named Abis Mal had found Jafar's lamp—and rubbed it. Jafar was back!

"You will help me get revenge on a certain street rat by the name of Aladdin!" Jafar commanded Abis Mal. The Rules of the Genie prevented Jafar from harming Aladdin himself. He promised Abis Mal a huge reward in exchange for his help.

Next, Jafar tracked down Iago. "I'm arranging a little . . . *surprise* for Aladdin, and your job is to lead him to the party," Jafar said to Iago.

Iago tried to resist. After all, he and Aladdin were just getting to be friends. But Jafar was more powerful than ever.

Iago had no choice. He went to Aladdin and

suggested that Aladdin take the Sultan for a scenic ride

on the Magic

Carpet. "And I . . .

I can take you to

the perfect spot,"

Iago added.

Aladdin

agreed. He had no idea that Jafar was there, invisible,

controlling Iago and leading Aladdin into a trap. Jafar

was watching Aladdin's every move.

Away they flew—Aladdin, the Sultan, and Iago—on the Magic Carpet. The Sultan was having the time of his life.

"Come on, my boy," he said to Aladdin. "Show me what this thing can really do!"

Only Iago knew about the danger that awaited them at their destination.

Back at the palace, Jafar made sure that Genie and Abu were out of the way. "I can't have any genies mucking about, ruining my plans," Jafar said evilly. He overpowered Genie, encasing him in a crystal sphere, and shackled Abu.

Then Jafar transformed himself into a small army of masked riders on winged stallions. Together, the riders and Abis Mal flew off and kidnapped the Sultan as he, Aladdin, and Iago lounged near the top of a giant waterfall.

Aladdin tried to
rescue the Sultan, but
Jafar's magic was too
strong. Aladdin fell
into the water and
was swept away by

the raging river. Then, just before Aladdin was thrown

against some jagged rocks, Jafar summoned his magic

. . . and spared his life!

"It is not yet time for the boy to meet his end,"
Jafar said to Abis Mal.

As Aladdin made his way home on foot, Jafar flew ahead to the palace to set the next phase of his plan in motion. In a palace dungeon, he held the Sultan, Jasmine, Genie, Abu, and the Magic Carpet captive. Then, disguised as Jasmine, he told the palace guards that the Sultan was dead, and that Aladdin was guilty of the crime!

Aladdin finally reached the palace, exhausted and worried about the Sultan. The guards immediately arrested him. At dawn, they prepared to execute Aladdin for the murder of the Sultan.

Meanwhile, inside the palace dungeon, Iago strained to lift the crystal sphere that held Genie. Iago wanted to regain Aladdin's trust. If he could just get the crystal high enough . . .

Crash! Iago dropped the sphere, shattering it. In a flash, Genie flew out the window and scooped up Aladdin before the executioner's blade fell.

Genie freed the Sultan, Jasmine, and the others. Now they just had to stop Jafar.

"You destroy Jafar's lamp, you destroy Jafar," Genie advised them.

Both Aladdin and Jasmine went after the lamp. But Jafar was on to them. And in his most powerful form as the evil genie, Jafar was a force to be reckoned with.

In his fury, Jafar ripped holes in the earth. Soon the palace grounds became a bubbling pool of hot lava. Aladdin jumped on the Magic Carpet and struggled to stay out of the fiery lava while chasing after the lamp. But mighty Jafar managed to keep it just out of Aladdin's reach.

Then, just when it looked as if Jafar had won, Iago swooped down and snatched the lamp.

"Traitor!" Jafar screamed, striking Iago with a fireball. The bird and the lamp landed on a ledge. With his last ounce of strength, Iago kicked the lamp into the fiery lava below.

"Noooooo!" screamed Jafar, as his lamp melted away and he began to spin faster and faster . . . until he disappeared forever!

It was official: Iago had definitely regained Aladdin's trust. And so the bird lived happily ever after, wallowing in luxury as Aladdin's "palace pal."

A Princess Pleads for Peace

It had been some time since Pocahontas had heard the sad news. Colonists from England had told her of Governor Ratcliffe's report that John Smith was dead. But still her sadness had not faded. Pocahontas felt confused and unsettled.

So, when
she got the
chance to sail
to England
to meet
King James,
Pocahontas

was glad. Maybe she could finally bring peace between
her people and the English. Soon Pocahontas and her
bodyguard, Uttamatomakkin, were bound for England
with a colonist named John Rolfe.

Once in London, Pocahontas was entranced by the hustle and bustle of the city. But then she spotted a villainous character from her past: Governor Ratcliffe!

"The king has appointed me to lead an armada against the savages," Ratcliffe announced to Pocahontas and John Rolfe. "The king wants his gold."

"There *is* no gold," Pocahontas argued. She

appealed to
John Rolfe.
They had to
speak to King
James and
stop Ratcliffe,

or there would be war in Pocahontas's homeland!

John Rolfe rushed to the palace. He asked King James to meet Pocahontas.

"Rolfe," the king replied, "you will bring her to the Hunt Ball. Prove to me she is as civilized as you claim, and I will stop my armada. If not, the armada sails."

At first, John Rolfe was concerned. Pocahontas didn't know English customs. Could she impress the king? But Pocahontas was willing to do anything for

peace. After
dance lessons
and a wardrobe
change, she
was ready.

"You look

beautiful," said John Rolfe when he saw Pocahontas in her gown.

He was not the only one who was charmed. At the ball, Pocahontas flattered King James, delighted Queen Anne, and twirled gracefully across the dance floor. At dinner, she sat in the seat reserved for the king's guest of honor.

But then the entertainment began. Ratcliffe brought out a wild bear, chained and muzzled. Clowns poked and prodded the bear with tridents.

"This is torture!" Pocahontas shouted, running to the animal's aid.

King James did not appreciate Pocahontas's outburst. He ordered the guards to lock her up, along with her bodyguard, in the Tower of London.

That night, as John Rolfe stood in his garden, wondering how to help Pocahontas, a hooded figure jumped over the garden wall. It was John Smith! Ratcliffe had lied to everyone! John Smith was alive, and he had heard that Pocahontas was in trouble.

Together, John Smith and John Rolfe devised a plan. They disguised Smith as a new

prisoner, slipped into the Tower of London, and found Pocahontas's cell.

"John Smith!" Pocahontas said with a gasp. "I-I thought you were dead!"

"Greatly exaggerated," Smith replied with a grin.

John Rolfe and John Smith fought their way out of the tower and rescued Pocahontas and Uttamatomakkin. When they were safe, John Smith explained what had happened to him. Ratcliffe had convinced the king that Smith was a traitor. When Ratcliffe reported him dead, Smith thought it best to stay hidden — or face execution!

But Pocahontas decided she would not hide from the king. She had to stop the armada! She marched into the court of King James and insisted that she be heard. She tried to convince the king not to attack her people.

"There is nothing to be gained," she said, "but much to be lost. For all of us."

Queen Anne understood. "There is no gold . . . is there?" she asked.

But King James remained confident. He said, "Ratcliffe assured me—"

"That I was dead?" said John Smith, stepping into the court.

Then the king saw the truth. Ratcliffe had lied about everything.

At the king's orders, John Smith, John Rolfe, and Pocahontas raced to the harbor to stop the armada before it set sail. Ratcliffe saw them coming. He ordered his men to cast off. But John Smith, on horseback, leaped off the pier and landed on the ship's deck.

John Rolfe and Pocahontas followed, and together John Rolfe and John Smith fought the sailors. They found Ratcliffe. After a heated sword fight, John Smith had Radcliffe at sword point. Ratcliffe pretended to give in, then reached into his cloak and pulled out a pistol!

"Good-bye, Smith!" Ratcliffe said with a sneer as he squeezed the trigger.

Just then, John Rolfe released the ship's yardarm.

The massive wooden beam swung across the deck, knocking Ratcliffe

overboard. He surfaced to find King James and his guards onshore, waiting to arrest him.

The armada had been stopped! John Smith's name was cleared. King James even gave him a ship of his own. Smith was free to travel the world in search of new adventures. And he wanted Pocahontas to go with him.

However, Pocahontas politely turned him down. John Smith understood

why: she was in love with John Rolfe.

But where *was* John Rolfe? Pocahontas couldn't find him anywhere—not even as she prepared to board a ship for home. Didn't he at least want to say good-bye?

Saddened, Pocahontas boarded the ship. It pulled away from the dock. Then, a voice behind her said, "Well, perhaps one day we'll return to London." It was John Rolfe!

He and Pocahontas stared into each other's eyes and pressed their hands together as they sailed on to the west. "Let's go home," said John.